First United States publication 1974
All rights reserved.
   Printed in the
United States of America.

L.C. Card 73–8003
ISBN 0–690–00276–9
0–690–00277–7 (LB)

Shawn Goes to School

by PETRONELLA BREINBURG
with illustrations by ERROL LLOYD

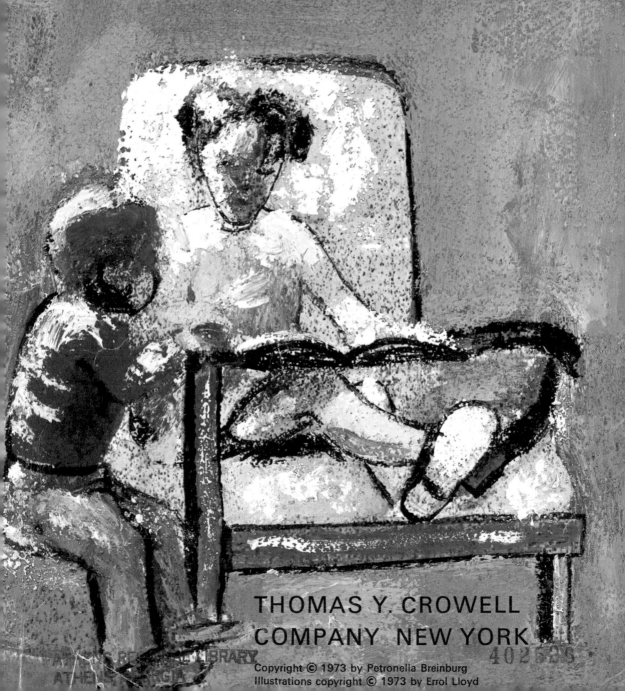

THOMAS Y. CROWELL
COMPANY NEW YORK

My brother Shawn always wanted to go to school.

He was sad when I went to school each day.

Then one day Mom and me
took him to the nursery school.

But Shawn didn't
seem to like it much.

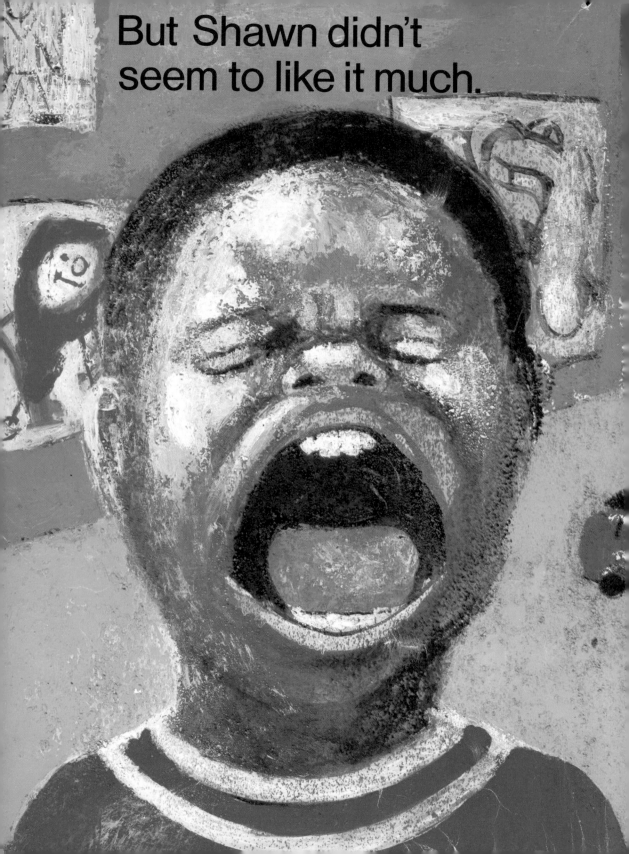

He wouldn't play
with anyone.

And when Mom and me
said Good-bye to him,

Shawn cried.

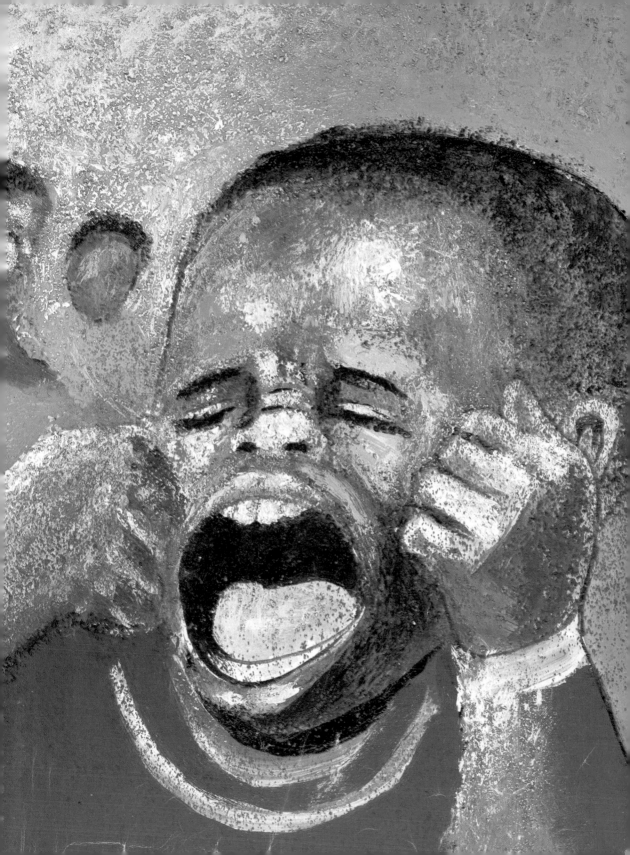

So we stayed awhile.
The teacher was kind.

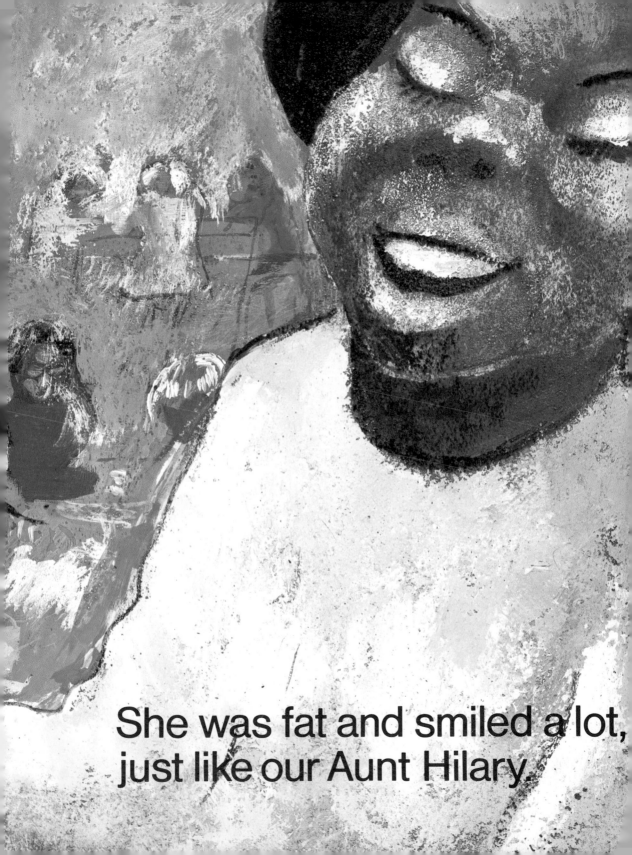

She was fat and smiled a lot,
just like our Aunt Hilary.

"We've got lots of nice kids,"
said the teacher
to Shawn.

"And there are lots of toys," said Mom.

"And they've got
a swing, too," I said.

"And a donkey for riding,"

said a boy who
wanted to be friends.

Shawn smiled
a teeny weeny smile.

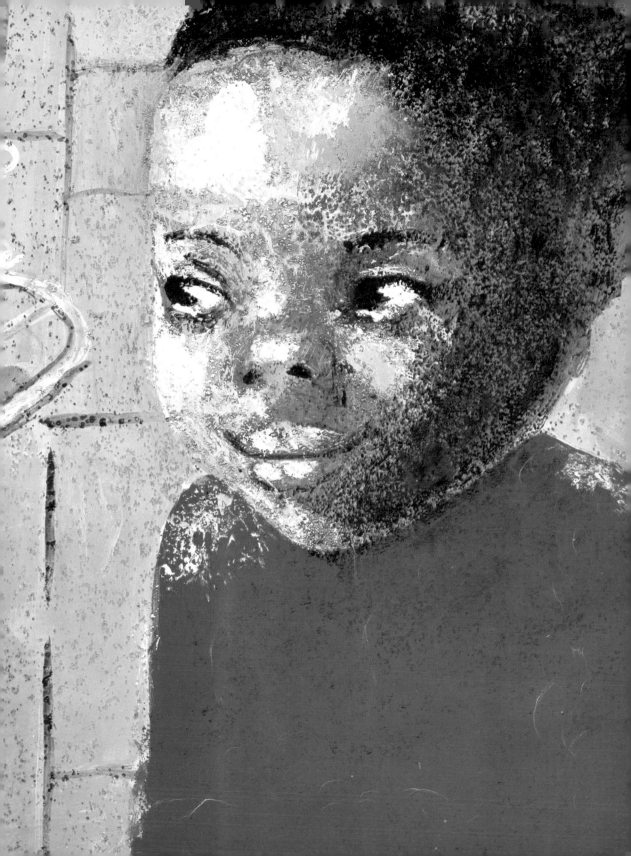

So Mom and me
left him at school.